We're Very Good Friends,
My Father and I

P. K. Hallinan

With special thanks to dads everywhere.

ISBN 0-8249-5375-4 (case)
ISBN 0-8249-5376-2 (paper)

Published by Ideals Children's Books
An imprint of Ideals Publications, a division of Guideposts
535 Metroplex Drive, Suite 250, Nashville, Tennessee 37211
www.idealspublications.com

Printed and bound in Mexico by RR Donnelley & Sons.

Library of Congress CIP data on file.

10 8 6 4 2   3 5 7 9

ideals children's books™
Nashville, Tennessee

We're very good friends,
My father and I.

We like to play catch

And watch trains roar by.

And sometimes we'll sit
At the base of a tree
And talk about places
We wish we could see.

Or sometimes we'll walk,
And we won't say a word.
But that's okay too
For good friends to do.

We like to play sports,
My father and I,

Like tennis

And horseshoes

And fishing with flies.

In winter we'll go
For a romp in the snow!

In summer we'll play
At the beach the whole day!

But then there are times
That we just sit and stare
At far distant stars
That light the night air.

We really like stars,
My father and I.

And always we're happy
Just being together
Like clams in the sand
Or birds of a feather.

And we like to play cards.

We even like mowing
And hoeing the yard.

But once in a while,
We'll just take a drive
And feel all the gladness
Of being alive.

We always have fun,
My father and I.

Then in the evening
We usually stand
Alone in the kitchen
And talk man to man.

And I see in his eyes
How deeply he cares,
And I hear in his voice
All the feelings he bears.

My father's my teacher;

He's my leader, my guide.

And I like being with him,
Right there at his side.

He's helped me to grow
And to stand very tall.

And I know in my heart
He's the best dad of all!

So I guess in the end,
Love's the best reason why . . .

We're very good friends,
My father and I.